Dora in the Deep Sea

by Christine Ricci
illustrated by Robert Roper

Ready-to-Read

Simon Spotlight/Nick Jr.

New York   London   Toronto   Sydney   Singapore

Based on the TV series *Dora the Explorer*® as seen on Nick Jr.®

SIMON SPOTLIGHT
An imprint of Simon & Schuster Children's Publishing Division
1230 Avenue of the Americas, New York, New York 10020
Copyright © 2003 Viacom International Inc.
Manufactured in the United States of America

4 6 8 10 9 7 5
Library of Congress Cataloging-in-Publication Data
Ricci, Christine.
Dora in the deep sea / by Christine Ricci ; illustrated by Robert Roper.— 1st ed.
p. cm. — (Dora the explorer ready-to-read ; #3)
"Based on the TV series Dora the Explorer(tm) as seen on Nick Jr."
Summary: Dora and Boots go down deep into the sea in a submarine to help Pirate
Pig find his lost treasure chest. Features rebuses.
ISBN 0-689-85845-0 (pbk.)
1. Rebuses. [1. Buried treasure—Fiction. 2. Marine animals—Fiction. 3. Rebuses.]
I. Roper, Robert, ill. II. Dora the explorer (Television program) III. Title. IV. Series:
Ready-to-read. Level 1, Dora the explorer ; #3.
PZ7.R355 Dl 2003
[E]—dc22
2003010523

Hi! I am  DORA . This is  BOOTS .
And here is our friend,
 PIRATE PIG .  PIRATE PIG looks sad.
What is wrong,  PIRATE PIG ?

"I have lost my  !"
TREASURE CHEST

says  . "The
PIRATE PIG   TREASURE CHEST

fell off my  and
SHIP

into the  !"
SEA

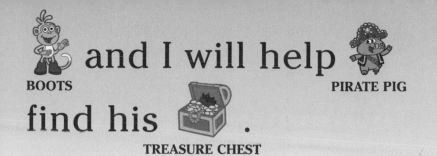

BOOTS and I will help **PIRATE PIG**

find his  .

TREASURE CHEST

Will you help too?

We need something to take us down into the 🏝️ .

SEA

What can take us into the 🏝️ ?

SEA

A  can take us down
SUBMARINE

into the ⬭ !
SEA

Ooh, we are going down into the  .

SEA

Look! A  !

SAND CASTLE

Hello, ! !

KING CRAB

There is a  with
FISH   SPOTS
by the   .
ROCK

I see a  **STARFISH** . . . and a funny clownfish!

Boots spots a  **GREEN TURTLE**.

Pirate Pig sees **YELLOW SEA HORSES**.

Oh, no! Here come some

 !

LOBSTERS

They will try to pinch

the  with their  !

SUBMARINE   CLAWS

We drove the  **SUBMARINE**

past the 🦞🦞 ! **LOBSTERS**

Now we need to find

the 🎁 . **TREASURE CHEST**

Hooray! We found the  !

TREASURE CHEST

But we have to watch out for  .

SWIPER

He will try to swipe the 🧰 .

TREASURE CHEST

Do you see  ?

SWIPER

Look!  is behind the !
SWIPER   WHALE

He is going to swipe

the !
TREASURE CHEST

We have to say " , no
swiping!"

SWIPER

Yay!  PIRATE PIG has his TREASURE CHEST !

Thank you for helping!